"FORGET
FEARS N[...]
HAVE A F[...]
NIGHT."

CYPRIAN EKWENSI
Born 1921, Minna, Nigeria
Died 2007, Enugu, Nigeria

First published in *Lokotown and Other Stories* in 1966.

EKWENSI IN PENGUIN MODERN CLASSICS
Jagua Nana (forthcoming)

CYPRIAN EKWENSI

Glittering City

PENGUIN BOOKS

PENGUIN CLASSICS

UK | USA | Canada | Ireland | Australia
India | New Zealand | South Africa

Penguin Books is part of the Penguin Random House group
of companies whose addresses can be found at
global.penguinrandomhouse.com.

Penguin
Random House
UK

This edition first published 2018
001

Set in 10.25 / 12.75 pt Dante MT Std
Typeset by Jouve (UK), Milton Keynes
Printed in Great Britain by Clays Ltd, St Ives plc

ISBN: 978–0–241–33984–8

www.greenpenguin.co.uk

MIX
Paper from
responsible sources
FSC® C018179

Penguin Random House is committed to a
sustainable future for our business, our readers
and our planet. This book is made from Forest
Stewardship Council® certified paper.

Glittering City

The girl standing on the railway platform turned as Fussy Joe approached. He saw her face and decided: young, provincial, eighteen or nineteen at the most, tall for her age, elegant, a knock-out. She had the fair skin that went with most beautiful Nigerian girls, a clear skin that spoke of fresh fish from the waters of the River Niger and palm oil from the plantations. Her eyes with their keen and inquiring look gave her away as a stranger in the city.

Fussy Joe stopped a few paces from her. For a provincial girl she dressed with charm: a greenish-blue blouse cut with a low neckline, emphasizing her small breasts. The short sleeves displayed the smooth, round arms. Around her waist, Fussy Joe noted the georgettes that made her hips look fuller than they really were: definitely a girl for him. Her fingers toyed with the ends of the red scarf that hung carelessly over her neck.

Fussy Joe coughed. She gave him a sideways glance.

'Coming from a long way?' he said.

She looked at him carefully. 'Yes – from the north. Three nights in the train.'

'You must be tired.' He smiled. 'It's a long journey.'

She looked at him with interest. 'Were you on the train?'

'No – I've come to meet a friend.' He looked round vaguely. 'It appears he's not on the train today.'

'I – I'm also expecting someone.'

'A boy friend?'

There was a sincerity in her smile that moved him.

'Not a boy friend. My mother.' She smiled.

'Perhaps she doesn't know you're here,' Joe suggested.

'But I sent her a telegram.'

Joe shook his head. 'Some telegrams get there after your arrival!'

He stood smoking for a while, and suddenly he glanced at his watch, and said:

'Where d'you want to go?'

'I don't know the place,' she confessed. 'I haven't been to Lagos before.'

'Have you an address?'

'No.' She frowned. 'No need for an address when my mother would meet me here.'

'You will have to come with me before a policeman arrests you.'

She looked at him wide-eyed. 'Arrest me? Really?'

'For loitering. Don't you know loitering is not allowed in the city?'

'Oh! I don't want to be arrested.'

Fussy Joe waved his arm and a fleet of taxis drove up, forcing their noses against his trouser-legs. He chose the longest and said: 'Get in! . . .'

She hesitated. 'But –'

'Go in first,' he said. 'You can't stand there for ever. Your train came late by about eight hours. Your mother must have got tired and gone away. In fact – now that I come to think of it – I believe I saw your mother. Just like you,' he said, looking closely at her face. 'Big, too. Like you. Light skin like you. Right?'

She nodded. 'You saw her. We're like sisters.'

'I even overheard her call your name. Now what was it? Erm – Erm – Erm –'

'Was it Essi?' the girl said.

'That's right! Essi! – Ah! – There was a young man and he also left. We heard a bridge fell and your train would not come at all.'

She went into the taxi, slightly reassured. Fussy Joe saw that the tension was abating. These provincial girls were either totally obstinate or completely trusting.

'I'm Fussy Joe, so they call me.' He kept up a barrage of smooth talk calculated to divert her attention. From her answers to his questions he had a fairly rough idea where to go in search of her mother.

'Where are we going?' she asked.

'We'll try and trace your mother,' he said, 'and if we fail –'

He smiled. He had a gold tooth which gleamed even in the back seat of the taxi.

'D'you know the place?'

'I have some ideas. We'll try.' He gave an order in Yoruba to the taxi driver and turning to her smiled again.

3

He noted the slightest flicker of a doubt in her young eyes, but talked rapidly on about trivialities, sensing, probing, seeking an advantage.

The taxi swung northwards along Denton Street and swerved into Ebute-Metta. It came to a stop in front of a well-lit house supported by large pillars in the moonlight.

Fussy Joe walked up and made some inquiries. He came back and fired off more orders to the taxi driver. Round and round the suburb they drove, each time stopping in front of a likely house.

Fussy Joe would come out of the taxi, ask questions, then return to the girl dejected. At last she began to feel hungry and exhausted. When the taxi stopped and Fussy Joe said: 'We get down here,' she followed him mechanically. He paused to pay his fare and to take down her suitcases.

'Is this where my mother lives?'

'No,' he said. 'But you can rest here a while –'

She hesitated. The taxi driver winked at Fussy Joe. Joe winked back at him. The taxi drove off.

'You'll rest here and tomorrow we'll go to the offices and ask people who may know your mother. It's late now –'

'My mother! –'

Her excitement delighted him. She was so young and sweet, and so unspoilt. He placed his hand in hers and she took it. In the dark passage as they climbed the stairs, he put his arm about her under the pretext of helping her up, and he was quick to see that she did not object.

He opened the door of a room on the landing and let her in.

'Is this where you live?' she asked.

She glanced about the room, crowded with expensive chairs, a radiogram, a television set and objects of art. Her feet sank into deep pile carpets.

'Be very quiet,' he said. 'You need to relax. There is no hurry. You have come to Lagos –'

He saw fear in her widening eyes. 'I'm not going to stop here – Take me down – back to the station.'

'Just sit down and wait, Essi.' He had taken off his hat now, and was piling her suitcases on the settee. All the tales she had heard about the bad men of the city came crowding back. They were the exciting stories they whispered after lights out in the boarding-house.

'I have come to meet my fiancé,' she said. 'My mother must be looking for me – somewhere in the city. I must go. Get up and let's go.'

He was quite cool. 'What more can I do? If you're afraid of me, if you want me to leave, after all the help I've given you and without even making sure that I hand you over to your mother, I'll leave this place to you for the night. But I'm not going to have you loitering like a girl without friends –'

'No, no, no!' she said, as he took his hat and made a bid for the door.

'Well! I tell you, you'll get your mother and your fiancé. Relax. You've had a long journey. You are tired –'

'I want to go!'

He was mixing her a drink. He came across the floor with a tray, a bottle, and two glasses. She did not know when he

5

had put on a gramophone record, and now the music swelled in the room. It was the song-hit of the moment and everybody was humming it. He was humming it to himself. She paused and listened.

'I know that tune,' she said.

'It's lovely.' His yellow tie seemed to smile too.

He had left the tray on the little stool, and from the drawer had produced a trumpet. He placed the trumpet carelessly against his lips and his cheeks filled with air.

He played like Lucifer himself. The notes were clear and high and wailing. He seemed to put tears into his trumpet, and she sat there with her mouth half open, watching him. When he put down the trumpet, she sighed.

'You have not touched your drink,' he said, wiping the mouthpiece of the instrument.

She was still looking at the ceiling. The music had done something to her. She felt elated, transported to a strange world where people rode on air and wore white silk and smiled, and floated higher and higher in their lovers' arms to heaven. She came out of the feeling like a person re-emerging from dreamland. It was a strange new feeling, and it made her shy.

'It is wine,' he said. 'No alcohol. It's good for you.'

She took it from him and tasted it. It was sweet. She looked at him invitingly.

'You are very beautiful,' he said.

She had a baby face, and her eyes made him think of a young puppy: so trusting, so innocent.

★

Late that night, both of them came downstairs. Her head was drooping sadly, and he was very silent. He paused at the foot of the stairs and smiled at her. She smiled, but did not meet his eye. He raised his hand again, and like magic a taxi appeared. She went in and he followed, carrying a music-case. His tie was hanging loose and another cigarette dangled from his upper lip.

'Harlem Club,' he said to the driver.

'Where is that?' she asked.

'Oh! That's my club. Where I play.' He pulled at the cigarette. 'My brother owns the place. I go in when I like and come out when I like. But other people have to pay to get in. Ever been to a night club?'

'Yes,' she said, 'we have one in our boarding-house.'

He smiled. 'And your mother is the hostess, isn' it?' He leaned back and grinned at her. 'Now, listen! Forget all your fears now. Have a fling this night. You see? Life is short and must be enjoyed.'

His philosophy did not agree with all she had been taught since childhood, but there was little time to question it. The taxi stopped, and he handed her down. At the gate, the orderly smiled at him and allowed him to pass. They looked with curiosity at the girl beside him and one of them said:

'Fussy Joe! –'

'That's me!'

He touched the peak of his hat, and smiled.

The rest of the band had already played one or two numbers before he got there. There was some heated talk before he took his stand, and one of the band-men made a sly remark about the girl.

Essi sat at a corner under the trees, and a moment later one of the waiters brought her a beer and some biscuits. She looked around the Harlem Club. Such a variety of people: all tribes, all creeds, all races. There were politicians here, and transport owners, editors, lawyers, doctors, but the women formed by far the larger proportion of the patrons. Black women with heavy make-up and fixed expressions on their faces. Their nails looked to Essi like red claws, their breasts swelled beneath the shining silk. They jumped out when a rhumba was playing, twisting their hips and clapping. Some of them sat with their male escorts; lawyers, white managers – most of the men had come with their wives and were quiet, unobtrusive. It was relaxation time in the city, and they had secluded themselves, so to speak, from the entire world. Essi saw a group around a table, intent on listening to a speech being made by a man in a blue robe and peakless cap. Beer bottles on the table could be counted by the score.

'Fussy Joe!' said a girl.

'Fussy Joe!' said another girl. The band had just finished a number, and Joe was wiping his trumpet. 'Joe, come and buy me beer – Joe, come buy me chicken – Joe, my dear – Fussy Joe –'

She was shocked at their lack of inhibition. Joe appeared pleased with himself. He spoke all Nigerian languages and all the girls were on intimate terms with him. He was popular.

But not once during the whole evening did he play as well as he had done while accompanying that gramophone record in the house. She began to wonder whether it had been pure accident, or just plain luck.

'May I have a dance?'

Essi looked up to see a man bending over her table.

'I don't know how to dance,' she said.

'May I sit with you, then?'

'No! No, please. I came with somebody.'

He went away, and presently returned, followed by a steward carrying a large chicken.

'For you, please,' he said, and walked away.

'I – I've had my dinner –'

But he had walked away, and her protests fell on deaf ears.

Left alone, Essi began to wonder where all this was leading. She had followed a man she had never seen before, believing that his intentions were sane. But now that she had discovered his selfishness, why did she not go back home? In fact, what was the next step from now? She had forsaken her mother, her fiancé, and everything she had ever learnt at school. The magic of the glittering city had confused her. It was unlike her to be awake so long after midnight. To tell herself the truth she was enjoying it. The experience was so new, it fascinated her. The lights – blue, green, orange – were whirling round and round in her head. Surely, this was a dream? She would soon wake up and find herself in the late train from Kano, covered with coal particles, and smoke.

II

There was little time to think, because everybody was trying to crowd into the short space of one night as much enjoyment as possible, as though this was the last night on earth. Once or twice Essi actually found herself on the dance floor in the arms of the man who had sent her a chicken. How did it happen? She was listening with half an ear to his account of himself, and what he hoped to make of her in this city, if – his words were bubbles, and they floated all about her eyes and ears, and nose, and slipped away skywards. This was crazy. *If you marry me. If you be my mistress, if –*

Joe danced with every girl in the Harlem, but not once did he take her out on to the marble floor. She knew why. He must have thought her too shabby to dance with him. You could see that from the type of girls he spoke to. Those in chiffon and high-heeled shoes with ankle clasps. Their handbags gleamed, and jewels shone on their wrists and ears. They were chic.

But who was this man Joe? Suddenly she found that she could not answer one question about him. Was this how he lived his life? Just loafing? He didn't seem to have one serious thought in his life, and didn't bother about anything. Everybody seemed to know him, and he seemed to know everybody. Yet he appeared quite prosperous. The way his room was furnished said so. He had enough good looks to win him a scholarship to study acting, and he wore his clothes with an elegance and dash which marked him out even among professional men.

About 3 a.m., the band began to pack up. The only music in the Harlem came from the amplifiers at the far corners and Essi was yawning at its monotony. Most of the seats were empty now, and the waiters were collecting bottles. Essi heard the clatter of plates from an adjoining section, and she knew the kitchen section was tidying up.

Fussy Joe came towards her. He was rather cagey in his approach, as if he feared that one of his glamorous girls would laugh at him.

'Let's go, now.'

Essi got up.

'We're going to play at the Flying Ant.'

'Where is that?'

'It's another club –'

'A-ah! – Don't you sleep?'

'I did all my sleeping when I was an infant.' He took her hand. 'Good night! – Good night –' he hailed at the stewards.

But she did not go with him to the Flying Ant. At the door of the Harlem, two men were waiting. One of them had his hands thrust into the pockets of his white jumper over the *lappa*. The other wore police uniform, and they were chatting lightly. Essi was the first to recognize the man in the white jumper as her uncle. He, too, seemed to have recognized her, for he was staring hard, trying, no doubt, to disbelieve the evidence of his own eyes.

'What! –' His hands came out of the jumper pockets. 'Is this not Essi?'

'Uncle! – Excuse me, Joe –'

'Essi, when did you come? Your mother has been worrying all day about you. I told her you were not on the train. We went thrice with Franky, and Mama, but at last we gave it up.' He was searching her with his eyes. 'Who are you with?'

'Er –' She swallowed. 'Erm – He's a friend. He helped me to get my things from the station –' Her story did not appear to convince him.

He looked at Fussy Joe, and recognized his type at once. His face darkened. The rest of the band came out, bundled into a car, and with Joe, drove away.

Essi broke away from her uncle. 'My trunks! – my trunks! – my boxes are in his house –'

The policeman blew his whistle, but the car did not stop. He turned to the girl.

'Do you know where he lives?'

'No, sir!' She was crying.

'You don't know where he lives?'

'I don't know the place, sir.' Her tears were running hotly down that clear smooth skin. 'Oh –' A sob choked in her throat.

Uncle placed a comforting hand on her shoulders. 'Listen, Essi. You have been very foolish to trust such a man. He could go any length with you. He's not responsible. He doesn't bother if his wickedness spoils your whole life. What d'you think your fiancé will do if he knows where you've been this night? And with a stranger, too! – Oh, me! You know how hot-headed he is. I swear he'll find out this your friend, and it will go badly with him.'

'Uncle, he told me he would take me to my mother.'

'Oh, me! He will tell you anything. I believe we saw him at the station in the morning, too. He was wearing this same coffee suit. Don't you know there are many such people in this city? And what do they do for a living? Ask me! The liar! Imposing himself on an innocent girl from the provinces!' His rage was painful to see. 'Don't you know what the girls call such a person?'

She stared at him.

'I – I don't know.'

'You'll soon find out.' He sucked in his breath. 'You're yet new in Lagos. But I believe the word has something to do with *brain.*'

'O-oh! A Brainer!'

'You know the term?'

She nodded. She didn't want to confess that it was part of her after-lights-out education at the boarding-house.

The street had become suddenly empty and quiet. The music from the amplifiers had faded, and the lights were out in the Harlem. Night had now really come, even for the night clubs.

'What d'you propose to do now?' said her uncle.

'I don't know.'

'It's too late for anything now. Follow me.'

III

Fussy Joe did not return from his rounds of the night clubs until five-thirty next day, and then not alone. He smiled when he saw the condition in which he had left the room before he went to the Harlem. The wine was on the radio, the two glasses stood empty on the tray. Essi's glass still had a little colouring of red to it, showing her amateurism. 'Where is your wife?' asked the girl who was with him.

She wore a native dress. Blue seemed to be her favourite colour. Midnight blue, relieved here and there by milk-white ankle clasps, gold-beaded necklaces, gold bracelets and earrings. A delicate material woven in the sheerest gossamer of white wool, thrown across her shoulder here, girded about her waist there – she did not seem like the kind of person one would expect to meet in a night club. With her gentle smile she looked like a home-maker.

She said she was a sewing mistress. Her mother lived in Lagos. Her father lived in another suburb of the city. She herself had left school when her father and mother had quarrelled, and having nothing else to do had learnt tailoring at the hands of a seamstress, but she much preferred the Nigerian fashions.

He did not bother her about her life history, but she had been on beer all night, and had only just mixed it with brandy, a shot or two of whisky, and was rounding it off with sweet wine. It was enough to loosen anyone's tongue.

He told her he was secretary to a leading firm in an enterprising corporation, that he had gone to England as a delegate to interview their opposite number and had only just returned. They exchanged lies, each one knowing that the other one was putting up a good show and not worrying to check the facts. She was content to be with so phenomenal a musician, and so popular a figure as Fussy Joe. Joe promised to put her in touch with a friend of his who was looking for intelligent, attractive young ladies to put on his counter. She thawed under his compliments, but suddenly she appeared worried.

'Where is your wife?'

'My wife?' He smiled. 'She's not here.'

She appeared more at ease. 'I don't want anybody to scratch my face.'

'Has it been scratched once?'

She smiled.

'Don't fear,' he said. 'She will not come.'

Joe was grinning. There were at least three girls who answered to the description of his 'wife'. And the fun of it was that each of them believed that she was *the* wife. Lilli did not know of Ajuah, and Ajuah did not know of that one who wears a buba and cloth: he had forgotten her name. There were many more. He did not need to maintain them when his tongue still had a coating of sugar at least one inch thick. They liked him, they were sorry for him; why wouldn't they pay their way?

But of them all, Lilli was the nearest to him, because of their son Olu. Lilli lived outside the city area, away from all the noise and bustle, because of her health. Like most of the girls who so willingly fell for him while he toyed with their affections, Lilli was extremely good-looking.

Not very tall, yet perfectly made. Athletic and springy on her feet, except during the rains, when she usually went down with a touch of rheumatism. She was honest and dutiful to him, and he was deceitful, tricky, and untrue to her. His neglect of her was a sore point with Lilli's neighbours who often asked her why she chose to carry the cross that was Fussy Joe. She listened to them but remained Lilli, Joe's wife, and mother of Olu.

Lilli was to have married a Mr Ojutayo. He was an engineer, qualified in England, and all through his training had written to her regularly. He had given her a job in the Posts and Telegraphs as an operator just before he left.

There she met Joe. Joe used to come and see another girl there, but with his usual greed his eyes seldom left Lilli's face whenever he called. Gradually his visits changed their purpose and soon there was bitterness among the operators because Lilli was accused of having snatched Joe. Lilli didn't mind so long as Joe didn't mind.

Lilli told him about her fiancé. Joe expressed great surprise, but in actual fact Ojutayo was a class-mate of Joe's. He had shown exceptional brilliance in the secondary school days, and it was not surprising that he should secure a Government scholarship as he did. Joe maintained that there was no harm in Lilli having a good time now and again.

Joe's interest in any girl became more intense if he knew that she was engaged to a good friend of his. They started going out together, and Olu was born. Ojutayo vanished from the picture after that. He had not heard from Lilli for the last six months of his stay, and when he returned home his first call was on Lilli.

He spent only three minutes in her room. The baby was sleeping, and Joe had gone to play trumpet in a night club. Lilli was in tears, and his chest was heavy with repressed sobs. He was smiling and wishing her good luck by the time he put on his hat and drove away.

Lilli had suffered much at Joe's hands. She had loved him so much that she had made herself a slave to jealous passions. Never a week passed without her turning up in hospital with a bleeding nose or swollen ear. She was fast gaining a reputation as an aggressive girl. And all for Joe's sake. The nature of Joe's life had been a constant source of friction between them. She did not expect to reform him, but at least she expected him to direct his talents to better use. She did not see any future in the life of a band leader. Joe could speak convincingly, at least to women. He could play a trumpet. He knew a lot of the men who mattered in the city. Why then, did he choose this drab, dangerous and cheap life? Why not find a steady job? A mere band leader in the city had no status, no security. But Joe loved his music far too much to listen to advice.

She had told him to become serious, to accept his responsibilities as a father and become a man. He made new resolutions but women always destroyed his resolutions and he always ended deeper in drink, deeper in jazz, deeper in disillusionment.

Despite all this she loved him because he thought very highly of himself and was as jealous of Lilli as a lioness of her cubs.

'Who was that man?' he would ask, in their night club days.

'Which man?'

'The one who was whispering to you? What was he telling you? D'you think I wasn't watching?'

'He was just greeting me.'

'Now, don't speak to anyone. D'you hear? I'm your husband, and if I don't speak to a man you are not to.'

He would leave her abruptly in the middle of the dance floor and join the band. She would sit still, and when he had played and flirted with all the girls, they would go home together, speaking to each other through their noses.

At times, he would disappear for weeks after a quarrel, and she would never see him, or hear of him. When his finances ran low he would come sneaking in, unshaven, asking for a meal. She often wondered why she could not leave him, as the neighbours had said. She had tried it once, though.

They had had one of their usual quarrels over another man, and she was in tears.

'I don't want to see you again,' she cried.

'You can go: and go to the devil, I don't care.'

'You don't care, because you have many girls.'

'That is not the point, Lilli. I haven't got time for useless arguments.'

He put on his suit, perched his hat at an angle and with his trumpet under his arm, strolled off.

'You're not ashamed, going from one woman's house to the other.'

He was not listening.

'Women feed you; women sew your clothes. Women are going to kill you, in this Lagos: you bed-bug of a man!'

The bed-bug saps your blood, while you enjoy being sapped, but once you feel a burning sensation on your skin, it runs and hides under the bedclothes. So was Fussy Joe.

He left her and went away, because his father had given him a room somewhere in Ebute-Metta. He did not often stay alone in this room, where he had first taken Essi, and much preferred to come down and join Lilli in her country house. Many people who saw him practising on his trumpet thought he lived outside the city. It was the address he gave when he wanted to be naughty and knock the heads of Lilli and another girl.

Lilli was his 'wife'. They had had their ups and downs, but they were still tied each to the other, though not as strongly as before.

He looked at the new girl in blue. She was right. He did not tell her anything about Lilli, but he suspected that she must know a lot. When a girl is so crazy about you, it's no use asking where she got her facts. Facts were free for the asking. Pleasant facts, but more savoury still, unpleasant ones.

She was quiet. Everything seemed to interest her, and her eyes danced from one object to the other.

'Is that your wife?' she asked, picking up a photograph.

'My wife, my wife, my wife! Are you so jealous?'

IV

Joe got out of bed at about 4 p.m. next day. Something told
him that today was pay-day for Ajuah. He had a bath, put on
a clean shirt, his best tie, and the inevitable coffee suit. He
caught a bus for Lagos, and sat back, enjoying a cigarette.
Fussy Joe played a variety of parts. One had to play so many
parts. To some people he said he was a journalist, attached to
the *West African Sensation*; to others, he was a legal practitioner
negotiating the deeds on a certain property situated along the
Marina; to others he was a band leader, or a film star. It was
difficult to remember what he was expected to be at any particular time. This afternoon he would shed everything and
just be Ajuah's lover.

He got down at Tinubu Square, and straightened his coat.

'This way, sir,' said the taxi drivers.

Joe took no notice.

He flicked his cigarette-ash at them, and adjusted the brim
of his coffee-coloured hat well over his face. He wore his hair
long, so that it came over the back of his neck and down beside
his ears. It gave him an air of distinctive mystery. Down Broad
Street he entered a shop, and there was the girl he had come
to meet. He had never been known to make a bad choice. Ajuah
was a world-beater. Her skin was pale brown, her features were
carefully chiselled, so that they were tempting to the photog-
rapher or painter. She had large nostrils, thin lips, eyes bor-
dered with eyebrows curled derisively. She looked proud and
haughty as if to proclaim the royal blood than ran in her veins.

'Hello, Joe,' she said, and embraced him in the shop. Her eyes were dancing as she looked him over.

Joe smiled. 'Hello, darling.'

'You've kept me waiting.' It was not meant to be a reprimand. He could feel that.

'Ne'er min',' he smiled. 'We went for band practice – I'll tell you all about it –' He went to the door of the shop. 'Taxi –'

From one shop to the other they went and Ajuah paid the bills. She bought him the most expensive shirts and shoes, socks to match, under-garments. He was not satisfied until he had selected half a dozen ties from an exclusive Swiss store beneath the most exclusive hotel. 'Ajuah,' he said. 'Things might be all right with me soon.'

'Indeed?' Ajuah looked interested.

He must make her feel he was a good investment.

'Yes. I'll be going abroad soon.' He leaned back when he had made this astounding revelation, and drew a cigarette to add to its importance. 'I hate the whole idea, but when you're being forced, what can you do?'

'Oh, please, don't go! –'

'I've made up my mind.' He lit the cigarette. 'I must go. Just imagine! Three years' time, I'm back, with degrees. Then my Ajuah and I we'll be riding high.'

'It will be nice, but I don't want you to leave me.'

'I know why,' he said. 'I know why. D'you know the words of that song?'

She did not answer, and he said: 'No need to look so gloomy,

Ajuah. I'm not gone yet. Well – as you don't like it – I'll have to go for that interview –'

She looked at him. 'Which interview?'

'You know they've been bothering me to come and be development officer. That's Senior Service. More pay, free house, car allowance, etc. You won't need to take me shopping any more. Instead I will take you.'

'Really?'

'I didn't even apply for the job. But they want to send me to the East. That's the snag. I hate to leave Lagos – I'm a city boy.'

Ajuah never did anything else but listen whenever Joe began to weave his fantastic plans. She humoured him by pretending to believe. They were all about as true as the gold tooth in his mouth, but they were told with such charm and conviction, that they could still fool an old friend like Ajuah.

By the time they stopped in front of the last shop, he was humming the tune, 'Why do robins sing in December –'

If anyone in Africa was proud of his voice, it was Joe. At best it was a tinny imitation of a blend of Bing Crosby, Frank Sinatra, and Perry Como. But Joe believed he could give any of these world-famous figures a mile and still beat them.

He got out of the taxi still crooning, threw a penny to a boy who seemed to admire him, and held the door open for her to come out, while he paid the driver out of the loose change she had left in his care.

Ajuah entered a large shop with neon lights and a marble floor. She began searching for some material and did not

notice that Joe's entire outlook suddenly changed. His movements became electrical. He looked like a man in a witness-box
who is making a muddle of things and is seeing the door of
the jail-house staring him in the face. Sweat broke out over
his face. He brought out his handkerchief and took off his
glasses to wipe it off. What was he to do? He had just seen
Lilli in the shop.

'Excuse me,' he said.

This was no place for such a meeting. Lilli, enraged, walked
straight across the shop and put her hand on Ajuah's shoulder.
Joe stared at the two girls in horror.

'So you are the one keeping Joe from me?' The girl puckered
her mouth and looked at Ajuah from her toes to the delicate
kerchief on her head. 'No wonder. I haven't seen him for three
weeks.'

Ajuah looked back into the fiery eyes of the medium-sized
girl. A well-made girl, light on her feet, with a little boy cling-
ing to her skirts.

'Answer me!' Lilli stormed. 'You have money to buy
him shirts and shoes. I have none. But see this boy. He is our
son! –' There were tears in Lilli's eyes.

'You're wasting your time,' Ajuah said, with her most dis-
dainful look.

'What!' Lilli stood with both hands on her hips, her feet
astride. 'That's no answer!'

Ajuah was looking round in her proud manner. She made
a move to disengage herself and Lilli struck the first blow.

What happened in the next few minutes had to be left to

the police to find out: and they did. The fine was barely five shillings each. But the loss of dignity, the bruises to be patched up, these cost more than five shillings. Ajuah had to tell them in her office next morning why she was wearing a turban instead of a head-tie. The nurse in the hospital was too used to bandaging Lilli's ear to be impressed. He made no remark, but his smile seemed to suggest that other parts of Lilli's body would have provided more delicious feeding for Ajuah's teeth than her ear. Her arm, for instance.

Joe was disappointed after this. He was not seen in the neighbourhood of either Ajuah or Lilli for weeks on end. Other girls called on him now and again, but were told the same story. He went to play somewhere, and had not returned.

v

Joe's first sign of life was one night when he sat in a bus on his way to Lagos. His dark glasses heightened his air of mystery. He had just told someone that he practised Yoga. He spoke a bit on reincarnation, but when the questions were getting too searching, he said lightly that he preferred to abstract himself from time to time away from the bustling world and to meditate.

He heard the sobbing of a girl behind him and he turned.

'Hello,' he said, recognizing her.

She lifted her big eyes at him. They were red.

'Mrs Bop, of all people.'

There are certain things which leave a person stunned

because of their improbability. He had always believed that
Bop and his wife were the happiest couple on the Island. That
was why his advances had been met with icy coldness. But
now her shoulders were shaking, and suddenly – he felt sorry
for the girl.

'What is it?'

'It – it's my husband.'

'Why? What has he done?'

'Kicked me out.'

He couldn't get it yet. He pinched himself to make sure
that this, indeed, was his chance.

'Look here,' he said, 'you've got to tell me more about this –
let's get down at the next stop. This is not the right place – here
in the bus.'

The Hotel France was the last place Joe wanted to enter.
His record there was not enviable. Most of the tables were
already occupied, but there was one near the piano, laid for
three. A girl was seated here. She was young, not more than
eighteen or nineteen at the most, though she was so tall. Her
skin was nearer brown than black. It was clear and her eyes
were young and keen, and gazed around inquiringly like those
of a young puppy learning to walk.

It was Essi. Abruptly he left Mrs Bop. 'Excuse me – shan't
be a minute!'

His heart was bursting with joy as he tapped on the table,
and with arms akimbo, said: 'Essi!'

She saw him. 'Ah! Fussy Joe! –'

'Anyone coming with you?'

'No, I'm alone. You may sit down.' Her young eyes closed in a sweet smile. She had a baby face. She was sweet. He wondered now, with a pang of regret, why on earth he had not stood up for her that night when Uncle had snatched her away.

'Where have you been?'

A waiter edged in the menu between them. He was a stout man, and he had the words HOTEL FRANCE on his breast. There was not much to choose from. Joe had a weakness for steak. He waved at Mrs Bop to join them and suggested that everyone else should try steak rather than take a full-course dinner. Mrs Bop was not eating. No appetite.

He ordered, and his eyes went back to Essi's face. 'Go on, Essi! Tell me. Where have you been?'

'H'm – it's a long story. Where is your trumpet?'

'You still remember?'

She winked. 'That night? O! You were mad. Joe, I should have come to see you all this time, but I couldn't even guess the place. I'm always confused.'

'Yes. I too made many attempts to see you; but they said you had left.'

'I'm leaving soon.'

'Are you?'

'Yes,' she said.

'No more marriage?'

'No,' she sighed. 'My husband has sacked me –'

Mrs Bop was growing jittery. She had counted herself two minutes ago as the most beautiful girl in Africa and had

believed that for Fussy Joe no other girl existed. It was boring
enough to find herself neglected exactly a minute later. She
had sat there, with a burning face, listening to the tripe
between the two lovers. It was disgusting. From time to time
she shot Joe a glance of fire, but his face was made of asbestos.
Flames could not scorch him.

The waiter arrived with three plates and set them down.
Mrs Bop said: 'Nothing for me, thank you!' Joe took a fork
in his right hand. 'Go on, try – by the way, Mrs Bop, this is
Essi –' The two girls nodded at each other.

'Ah – Essi. You've not changed much.'

'Me? Don't you see how lean I am? My husband starved me
then beat me well, and now he has kicked me out – You did
well to hide. My uncle has been looking for you. Wants to take
you to court. He's an ex-police superintendent, and he never
gives up a chase – I'm still staying with him.'

'Mphm! –' said Joe, with his mouth full.

'That's all.'

'How d'you happen to be here?'

'When I was ill, a friend gave a party which I could not
attend. Now I'm well, and she says I must come here and dine
at her expense.'

'And see the coincidence! – Of course, I knew I would see
you again. I never lost hope.'

'And I, too –'

He looked at her again. She wore the same greenish-blue
blouse cut low in the neck, emphasizing her breasts. There
was a red-and-blue ribbon stuck above her left breast. Her hair

had been stretched and combed out, but it was cut short, and there was just one comb in it: near the parting. She parted it on the left. She breathed health and youth as she sat there. She was clean as fresh air and temptingly provincial.

'Essi, you look wonderful!'

Mrs Bop said, 'I should be leaving now. Thank you very much, Joe!' She got up, pushed back her chair, and walked out of the Hotel France.

Joe looked at Essi with his mouth wide open.

Essi smiled. 'Who is that?'

'Don't mind her. She's been following me about trying to borrow money off me. She's a damn nuisance. Her husband kicked her out, and she wants to hang on me. Who has the time?'

'Why don't you lend her some money? The poor girl.'

'She's not worth it.'

Essi turned round and he followed her gaze. Sailors were coming into the Hotel France in dozens. They came in their shore clothes and caps and sat at the other end of the bar reserved for drinks only. Joe was regarding them with searching eyes.

'The boat is here now,' he muttered.

'The boat?'

'No, no! – I was talking to myself.'

He stood up. 'Well! I must be going now.'

He was gone. She had not even asked him for her suitcases, or where he lived. He had not even taken an interest in all she had suffered simply because she had been stupid enough to trust him for a moment. What a heartless man he was.

It was he who had caused all her misery, and had ruined the entire purpose of her visit to Lagos. She had missed a husband for his sake, and he didn't even bother. Where were all the crazy promises he had made her on that first night? This was a time when she could do with the fulfilment of those crazy dreams, and he had left; without even leaving his card. Her vision was clouding over with tears; she tried to check her sobs.

She was jerked sharply back to the present by the voice of the waiter. 'Your bill, madam.'

She dried her tears on a handkerchief. 'My bill?'

'Yes, Ma!'

'You're making a mistake. He's gone.'

She rose too, and walked away.

The waiter stared after her until she was out of sight. 'Them craze,' he said. 'All of them. Them craze!' Having delivered this verdict, he rubbed his chin reflectively. 'That gal – what he dey cry for?'

VI

Joe walked down the Marina, whistling a gay tune. Far out on the lagoon, the large ocean-going vessels were anchored. He could see the lights in their portholes. Now and again, the breeze would waft in snatches of music from the decks.

He walked like a man acting for a cinematograph. His hands were thrust deep into the pockets of his coat, his shoulders were bowed, and his hat was pulled down over his face. He passed a lot of sailors, but there was one he was looking for. He wondered if he had come on this trip. If he had, things wouldn't be so bad.

Those flash ties and fancy socks he brought could make good business, to say nothing of the watches that escaped the eye of the Customs. Joe particularly wanted to see him because he had promised him a trumpet, and one or two instruments for the new band he was proposing.

At first, when he bumped into him he was not prepared for the shock.

'Hello, Joe! –'

Bill! – Bill the Sailor. He was a Norwegian, about the same age as Joe and he was tall and big with blond hair. He radiated good cheer. How he had come to work on an American boat, Joe had not quite bothered to find out. There must have been many boats in port today.

They walked along the Marina for a while.

'Now, where do we go?' Bill said.

'A drink first,' Joe suggested.

'Yes, I'm thirsty. Been drinking salt water all day long.' He laughed and Joe laughed too, slapping him on the back.

He still walked with a roll, as if trying to feel whether the earth were steady enough to support him. He was in white shorts, and he made eyes at every girl who passed under the street lamps, and there were quite a few of them. They knew when the boats arrived, and had come out literally on parade. Young ones, painted ones, carved ones, girls in silk, girls in velvet, women holding on to plastic handbags and wearing high-heeled shoes, women in Nigerian dress and women in frocks; he stared at them all as they passed. Once he whistled, and two girls came towards him.

He said, 'I'm sorry', and they returned to the shadows. But they still hovered around them till they had regained Broad Street and called at a bar frequented by sailors in port.

'Now, what will you have?'

Bill was all hospitality, and would not discuss business until he had lowered a couple or more mugs of ale. Joe knew that and did not rush him. He took out a cigarette but he paused with it halfway to his mouth.

'What's the trouble?' Bill asked.

'Er – Er – nothing.'

Joe had seen something. The bar was crowded. There were a lot of sailors, and girls, laughing, some dancing and tittering. Others flirted or sat around drinking peacefully. But Joe was not looking at any of them. He was looking at a man. The man had his back towards Joe, and he was systematically getting himself drunk. He shook his head from time to time, and repeated his orders.

'Whisky! –' Joe heard him shout.

It was Bop. He had turned his eyes suddenly, and they rested on Joe's. They were smoky eyes in that they tended to conceal the fire beneath. Mr Bop the band leader had never been known to drink even lemonade; and now he was raving mad.

He came towards Joe, and Joe could smell the fight in him. His first words surprised Joe.

'Here you are! – ha, ha, ha –' He smiled. 'Did you find her good company?'

Joe's mouth twisted.

'Who?' He was not specifically addressed, and he was surprised to find himself answering.

'My wife, of course,' Bop roared.

The words echoed through the entire bar. Everybody seemed to stand still. The barman opened his mouth. He was holding a glass he was polishing as if posing for a photo. Glasses raised remained where they were. Necks stiffened; but all eyes were on Joe and Bop. Interest and curiosity pulsated through the bar.

Bop was in the centre of the stage.

'You took my wife out and brought her here to the Hotel France to dine. You knew we had quarrelled. Am I wrong in asking you whether you found her entertaining company or not?'

The bar rocked with jeering laughter. 'Answer! –' some of the listeners urged, raising their glasses.

Joe was speechless. The sweat poured down in a stream from his eyes, ears and mouth. Wiping it off did no good. The handkerchief became sodden, and the sweat throbbed outwards, as if from a stream. He was merely smearing the sweat over his face. To everybody else the cool wind from the Marina was bordering on the chilly side. But Joe was on fire. His hands trembled. His collar crinkled. Bop had to admit that if he had hit Joe in the stomach, he could not have tortured him more.

He turned his back on Joe, and was about to return to the

counter when Joe followed him, half pleading, half threatening.

'Mr Bop – I take great objection – after all, everyone knows that you're my boss – I – I take – great objection to all this. Er – if you're quarrelling with your wife and I get to know, it's my duty to – er – settle the matter – I mean –'

He looked a comic. His arms were hanging low, and his suit was shapeless. His hair seemed to have been cut, so much had it shrunk from the dampness.

'Ha, ha!' – everyone was laughing.

Joe glanced round. He was alone, and the sailors had gone. The rest of the band-boys appeared from nowhere. Something about the coincidence aroused his suspicion. Mrs Bop must be a fast worker. She was on the warpath, was she? Such a woman could be indeed dangerous, and demanded instant discipline. It was not difficult to imagine what she had told her husband. 'That your friend, the one they call Joe. He saw me in the bus – and began worrying me – I just followed him to hear what he would say – and he calls himself your friend!'

The band-boys were laughing at him. They knew him for what he was. The *Brainer*: the glib inventor of lies, the city boy who was a victim of his own virility and codelessness. Fussy Joe's mouth hung open, for there, standing before him were Essi and Mrs Bop and the instrumentalists. Their laughter throbbed and drummed in his ears. This was hell on earth.

'Talk, now!' they urged. 'Talk!'

He did not talk, but the sweat continued to pour. His suit

continued to wrinkle. His anxiety was touching. Gone were all the studied movements of cigarette lighting, the careful curl of lip as he chose his words, the poses struck for effect. Only the man Joe was left: and he was no man at all.

The laughter was beyond him. He had gradually edged to the door and now, amidst a burst of final laughter, he gained the street.

'D'you know where he's going?' said Bop.

'No! —' said the band-man.

'Take my word. He's going to see Lilli. And, boys! what a yarn he'll spin her! —'

'Oh! —' groaned the band-boys.

VII

Bop had guessed right. Joe took a taxi. He was still sweating profusely, but he was set on seeing Lilli, this night or never. And he was going to tell her things.

The car was much too slow to keep pace with his thoughts. No car could have conveyed him fast enough to Lilli. He wanted to fly. He wanted to be there, just by taking thought. But having failed in all these as yet unperfected means of transport, Joe had to be content with twisting his face and cursing the driver all along the way.

He found Lilli cutting out a dress.

'Ha, Joe! Is this your eye? You ran and left me to fight in the shop before everybody – see my ear.'

'I'm very sorry, Lilli.'

'What's the matter?' she asked, sensing the misery in his voice.

Then she saw his clothes. She had never known him to look like this. Not even when he was rushed out of bed without a shave or a wash. You could always depend on him to look polished and clean. His hair was dishevelled. His shirt was sodden and clogged against his back. His tie was wrinkled. But worst of all – he was trembling violently. No girl would have fallen for him now.

'Lilli! –' he groaned, 'I have been fighting for your sake.'

'Fighting? Ha, ha! Joe to fight – and for my sake, too!'

He had to be cautious, if he was to achieve his aim. 'I'm serious, Lilli.' He took a seat. He was beginning to regain his composure. His hand went instinctively to his breast pocket for a cigarette, but he remembered now that his coat was at the bar. He had left it behind in a hurry. Or had he taken it off in the taxi? He did not labour the point. 'Get me a cigarette.'

Lilli, anxious to relieve some of the anxiety from her own mind, ran rapidly and returned with half a dozen sticks. He lit one carefully, holding it with the very tips of his thumb and forefinger, puffed for a long while, and blew a perfect ring towards the ceiling. He was once more in his element.

'Some people,' he said, 'some people don't know the limit. They think they can just go on talking. They don't know the law is there.'

Lilli was wondering what he was driving at.

'What is it now, Joe?'

'Don't mind that foolish Mrs Bop and the husband. Of course, Mrs Bop is not a street woman –'

Lilli jumped to her feet.

'She called me a street woman? Tell me! –' She jumped into her shoes, pulled down a new frock from the hanger.

'She did what! –' She was getting into the frock.

'No, no, no! – Don't take it like that.' Joe was cool now. 'You keep on telling me that I don't love you, that I neglect you. Now, look at me!' He stretched his crumpled shirt. 'Is this the Joe you know? And why am I like this? For whom have I made all this sacrifice? For my own Lilli, who doesn't even bother.'

'Tell me again – Mrs Bop called me – what?'

'I told you.'

'I shan't have it! – I shan't have it! She must come and prove it to the court. But she must prove it to me first!'

Joe smiled. He had sown the seed of disruption. There was nothing to do now but sit back and watch. To judge by Lilli's feverish dressing-up, things would be done tonight that would be talked of for years.

Lilli was ready now.

'Where is she?' Lilli asked. 'Where did you leave her?'

He named the bar, and added: 'But perhaps she has gone home with her husband! Heh! – Ha, ha!'

He strolled out on to the street. He was not quick enough to duck, because Bop had already seen him. He put on a penitent smile, and even ventured to extend a friendly hand.

'Mr Bop, I'm sorry about what happened. You see, these girls. I do not really er –'

'What did I say? I knew you would come here and incite Lilli. What stories have you been telling her?'

'None whatever.'

Lilli came out then in a rage, and at first would not speak to Bop. But she soon noticed that the two men were literally arm in arm, embracing each other, while a sly expression of intense cunning twisted Joe's face.

'Oh, the trumpet,' Joe was saying. 'Sure, sure! – I'll let you have it at once. Sure – shall we go by taxi?'

'The sooner the better.'

Lilli gasped. She saw the two men get into a taxi and drive off. Joe had not said another word to her. She would have gone to make a fool of herself as she always did.

In the car, Bop gave Joe his first shock.

'The police are looking for you,' he said.

Joe's throat contracted.

'Me? Impossible,' he smiled.

Fears crowded fast in his mind. His greatest fear in life was that his end would be brought about by a woman. He wondered what Mrs Bop had been telling the police.

'Yes, you! – Zeine was arrested a few moments ago.'

'My sailor friend? So that's his real name? I called him Bill.'

'Well, Bill! He had been drinking for some time, and then he left the pub with that girl who calls herself Rose. They did not know that one man was shadowing them. When they took a taxi, he took one. Just as they were stopping in front of her house, his own taxi pulled up, and he challenged them. He was a CID man.'

'I knew that,' Joe mumbled.

'Wait! You'll see how you come in. He told them they were under arrest, and the man Zeine did not want any trouble. What did he do? He brought out five pounds and offered it to the CID man. The man didn't believe in being corrupted. Then Zeine changed tactics. He said he had a licensed guide, and he mentioned your name.'

Joe swallowed. 'My name?'

Fussy Joe had told Bill that he was a licensed guide, and the gullible sailor had believed him.

'You're a licensed guide, are you not?' Bop asked.

'Yes, yes,' he said. 'I – er – I am a licensed guide. Hem!' he frowned.

Bop was silent for some time. And then he said suddenly: 'D' you know Ajuah is in hospital? That girl! Lilli did things to her.'

'Ajuah?'

'Yes, Ajuah. You went shopping with her the other day, didn't you? Lilli ought not to have been so free with her blows. The charming girl might lose her eye. So I'm told.'

'Oh –'

'You should go and see her. It will keep your mind on your own girls –'

'Don't mind the wretch.'

'Ajuah, a wretch! – Fussy Joe!'

'She's been pestering my life.'

'How?'

'Well, I don't like girls who keep asking for money all the time.'

'So Ajuah was depending on you. I heard it was the other way round. Of course, you can't believe the gossip of these girls. It's all false –'

Joe's eyes were getting red with anger.

He hated Bop. The man knew far too much about him. Even if Bop promised to give him all the band's takings every night for the next two years, he resolved never again to play that trumpet for him again. The man was infuriating. He never said anything that did not have a double or triple meaning. Who told him all he knew? People must have been talking too much about him. His head was in a whirl. All this gossip, and then the police after him.

He was relieved when the taxi drew up under the mango tree. Bop preceded him up the stairs. As he came up behind the band leader, he found that there was someone standing at the door. Her keen eyes danced. It was Essi.

'Hello, Essi,' he grunted.

'I want my suitcases,' Essi said.

'Why? Why is everybody against me?'

He took the key out of his pocket and opened the door. The room was in disorder. Essi went in last, and she sat on the sofa.

'Oh! –' she exclaimed suddenly. 'I nearly sat on this!'

'What's it, let's see.'

Bop tried to get them from Essi, but Joe was quicker.

'They are my wife's earrings,' he said. 'Let me have them.'

Joe slipped the case into his pocket. He reached for the trumpet and handed it to Bop, complete with case.

'Anything more?'

Bop laughed. 'All in good time!' He opened the case, blew a note or two, and checked the instrument over. Then he replaced it in the case. At the door, he paused and said over his shoulder. 'Look, Joe. I have no malice against you. If you have any sense in your head, better quit. Everything is against you. People have become wise to your lies. Better think hard.'

'Thank you,' Joe slammed the door after him. 'Bother! He doesn't know that by just doing that! –' and he snapped his fingers – 'I can make him starve!'

'Mm? Can't he play elsewhere?'

'I tell you the Harlem Club is owned by my own brother. Don't you remember the night we went there?'

'Where are my suitcases?'

'Essi, you're not going anywhere now. You must stay here for some time.'

'No, no, no! If you don't give me the suitcases, I'm going away. You can eat them.'

'You haven't told me where to find you.'

'Don't worry.'

She had seen the suitcases and she went and took possession of them. Suddenly her mouth widened. The boxes were weightless.

'What happened?'

'Oh, I sent your clothes for cleaning.'

'Who begged you?'

'I thought it was a good idea.'

Essi did not know what that meant. 'When do you expect them back?'

'In a week or two.'

'I should be gone by then.'

'I'll send them to you.'

Her heart was heavy. That trunk contained all her best clothes and trinkets: the pick of her garments which she was taking to the house of her husband.

She did not know, until later, that Joe had sold all her things and spent the money. It was all part of the routine of making a living as a Brainer.

Joe knew all the *Paro* or discount men and never hesitated to make full use of them. They took very little commission and would sell anything for you within a month, and give you cash.

Essi did not say anything. Her hands were tied. She could not speak. To whom could she turn? To her uncle? That would be too noisy and scandalous. To her mother who had denied her? This was just a part of the price she had to pay for the lesson her youth was teaching her. It broke her heart. She began to cry. It was like a baby crying. The keen eyes filled and the tears ran down her smooth cheeks. Joe was moved.

He tried to put his arms around her, and something hit him on the face; then on the head.

'But, Essi!' he muttered, as he slid to the floor.

Essi replaced the torchlight and walked out on him.

VIII

Unseen forces were moving beneath the traffic lights of Lagos City. Joe did not know it at the time, but the wheels of fortune were rolling him towards the sea. Plans for his destruction were already in progress and some of them were in operation.

Not long after Joe left Lilli's lodgings a police van drew up, and Lilli answered certain very disturbing questions.

'No,' she said. 'I haven't seen him for three weeks. A long time now – yes, we quarrelled.'

'You're sure?'

'A-ah! One of your men arrested me. I paid five shillings for "disturbing the peace", or what you call it.'

'Oh, yes. If you see him, will you let us know?'

The sergeant went outside and the van slid off. As soon as she was back in the room, Lilli's bravery left her. She began to cry. Who was causing all this? Surely, Joe had wronged somebody. The police had never come here since he moved to the countryside. Neither had Bop ever asked Joe to return his trumpet. Joe had been with the band ever since she knew him.

They were jealous of him, that was all. Even the policemen. They did not like to see him in his fine clothes with wonderful girls they could not get. It hurt their pride. What had he done? If he was a liar, a cheat, had he not been that all these years? Why the sudden interest? And how did the police expect her to give her own man away?

Lilli pulled herself together. This was no time for tears. She must save Joe. If she saved him, and he still would not learn his lesson and leave the company in which he was involved, that would be his funeral. She would try to make him a useful man to society. O Lord! she prayed. If only he would escape. This must be something serious indeed. She recalled how the sergeant had twisted his face when he asked: 'Have you see Joe?'

He would be glad if Joe got into trouble. He himself had proposed love to her and she had jilted him. She knew them all. Put Joe in jail, and they would be the first to laugh at her. She lay on her pillow weeping, trying desperately to think of a way she could help Joe. First thing was to be near him. She got up, wiped her eyes, and put on some make-up.

She caught a bus to his lodgings. She walked neatly and without any sign of haste, trying to suppress the excitement that burned within her.

She met Essi just coming downstairs as she went up to Joe's room; but this was no time for jealousy. It was a time of crisis, and they would all fly away from Joe.

She found him seated on the divan, without his coat and with his head in his hands. When he saw her, he stopped groaning and tried to look unruffled. He began to spin her a yarn about the girl who was just leaving.

She cut him short.

'Joe,' she said, 'the police are looking for you. They came to my house in the van.'

'Looking for me?' His eyes darted about the room. He got up.

'There is no time to be lost,' Lilli said. 'They may be here any

43

minute. Dress up. If you have some money, take it with you. Quickly! We're going somewhere. Then we can find out –'

'I haven't any money,' he said. 'A friend promised to give me two hundred pounds –'

She paced about the room impatiently while he got himself ready. She opened her handbag, shut it. She stopped abruptly, her ears cocked.

'Oh, hurry up! –'

He was ready. He had his hat on, and a desperate look was on his face.

'Let us go. Anywhere! Just to gain time to plan.'

'Joe, what has caused all this? Have you done anything strange? Why are the police looking for you?'

He told her nothing. 'It's persecution,' he said.

'Oh, Lilli! –' he sobbed and held her close.

'Joe – dearest Joe! –'

'I have been a fool! I have been a fool –'

Her face was wet against his, her shoulders shook in his arms. He held her close, and made promises he had never made before; and he meant them.

'Lilli, you were always telling the truth, I never listened. I just thought you were jealous.'

'It was a woman – who d-did this!'

Her sobs choked her, and she rocked on her feet. 'What a fool I have been!'

Joe said. 'Why did I not drive away all those girls? I allowed them to involve you in all this. Oh! –'

To her, he said: 'Where's Olu?'

'He's at home. At home! The poor boy. He doesn't know what's going on. He's sleeping.'

'Good for him. I give him my blessing.'

'You must not talk like that, Joe. We can still do our best.'

He took her downstairs. There was no time to be lost. He raised his arm in the usual manner, but the magic had gone out of his call, and no taxis arrived. He went towards the park.

The park was a hundred yards away, and he saw the boys cleaning their cars. None of them appeared to recognize him: he wondered why, and he suddenly felt how empty his power over them had been. He took off his hat in the mocking manner that never failed to amuse them, but they turned their backs on him.

'Don't you know me again?'

'What is it, *Oga*?'

'I want a taxi!'

'They are all booked.'

'What are you talking?' He was smiling. 'Here is your money! Lilli, give them some money.' Lilli gave him a sheaf of pound notes from her handbag.

He flourished them, but nobody paid any attention to him. He looked around him. In the distance he saw – just a glimpse – a police car. It was trying to overtake a red bus. It was approaching the park. As they watched, it swung into the taxi park. In a minute, he had jumped into one of the cars.

'Here, Lilli – quick! –' Lilli darted forward suddenly. Her shoes and handbag made her clumsy. She leaned her arm against the door, squeezed her body in – some of the onlookers began to understand. They shouted: 'Thief! Thief! Stop him!'

Not minding the other drivers who were getting into their cars, Joe swung out. He wove his way through the traffic like a snake and slipped through the level-crossing a split second before the gateman closed the gate against all comers. Beyond the gate, he abandoned the car and watched the goods train pass. He was counting the wagons.

'Thirty! – Thirty-one! –'

Lilli said: 'Where do we go now? Is no use, Joe. Let's give ourselves up!'

He took her to the other part of the fence, got a boat, took off his coat, and began a leisurely journey across the lagoon.

'All this suffering because of Mrs Bop! What did you see in her?'

He said, 'It was bound to be a woman. I knew a woman would finish me.' What he needed was time to get away and think. It was no use getting into police hands now.

He came ashore at Ebute-Ero market and made his way to the Marina with Lilli close beside him. In moments of trouble, Lilli was always near. But this time, he wanted to excuse himself, because he had some very secret call to make. There was no way of getting rid of her.

He stood under the trees for a time, impatiently watching the labourers at the Customs. Lilli pleaded with him to move on, but stubbornly he waited till the man he wanted came towards him from the Customs shed. He came unobtrusively and greeted Joe.

Joe said: 'I want that dough now.'

'He hasn't given me yet.'

'What are you talking?'

'I say I haven't seen him.'

'Haven't you got anything?'

'What of this?'

The big man looked about him, dipped his hand into his robe and produced a fat wallet. He extracted something from one of the pockets. 'Count this,' he said. 'I think it is ten pounds.'

'Ten pounds! Out of two hundred.'

'Don't count it here. They're watching us.'

'Okay, I'll see you.'

Lilli wanted to know who the man was, why he was paying Fussy Joe money, who was watching them. Were they doing anything crooked? But as soon as Joe got the money, he took Lilli's hand, and mixed with the crowd.

The money felt good in his hip pocket. Ten pounds was better than nothing, but it was not enough to get him out of Lagos for a while. Why were people becoming so wise nowadays? Joe had told a trader named Akande that he had a dozen bales of cloth to clear from the Customs, but was short of ready cash. Akande had promised to come in on the deal, provided he could get the goods at a big discount. Joe had agreed, shown him the forged invoices, and the expiry date, when the goods would be auctioned. Akande looked simple enough.

'I will bring de money,' he had promised.

Joe had reckoned on getting the two hundred today through his labourer agent.

He stopped suddenly.

Lilli said, 'What is it now; let's go! –'

'That fellow has cheated me,' Joe said, 'I'm going back!' He was sure that the trader had paid the two hundred. He must have handed it over. 'Come along, Lilli, let's go!'

He dragged her through the maze of people and lorries, but from a distance he saw a police van. The man he sought was being questioned: a crowd had gathered. Joe turned to Lilli.

'Off we go, Lilli.'

He spun through the crowd. On Broad Street he joined a funeral procession, leaving them at St John's Church. But there was a man who detached himself from the crowd the moment Joe and Lilli left the church.

The man came towards him as he entered a taxi. He saw the watch on the man's wrist, and the set expression on his face. He was in plain clothes, but Joe knew he was a policeman.

'Don't show me your card, please,' Joe said. 'And don't try to arrest me, because I ain't done nothing.' He shoved Lilli into the back seat, plugged the taxi driver's fist with a sheaf of notes, pushed him aside and took the wheel.

The taxi turned into Broad Street. Escape at last. He was angry to note the heavy traffic. It was madness to edge along the queue of cars, and swing into Balogun Street. Smoke lay behind him as the car zipped along Ereko Street. He saw the expression of surprise on the faces of the men, and he knew they must have thought him mad to drive so fast.

Up Carter Bridge. If they got him, six months' imprisonment, plus six strokes of the cane. Unlicensed Guide. Carter Bridge behind: down Iddo. Unlicensed Guide. Buses – passengers bustling to get into the Kano train – market women selling onions, eggs, just arrived from the north – handcarts loaded with yams – more policemen trying to stop him while they took in details about an accident which had just occurred. Unlicensed Guide. He did not listen. Other cars were stopping, but he disregarded the signals and cut through.

'Stand if you dare!' he shouted to the man who tried to stop him.

Just bordering on Denton, and near Oyingbo he saw a man with a hand-cart trying to cross the street. In a flash – without time to think – Joe swung the car and slammed on his brakes. It was too late. The shriek of his tyres was drowned by the yell of the onlookers. All women raised their faces and their arms in supplication.

Cars and buses stopped just short of ramming one another. The street was in confusion.

Joe's car had somersaulted and by the time they got it on its wheels excitement was uncontrollable.

A stretcher appeared, and the two bodies found places on the shelves of an ambulance. The crowd hummed as they watched the large red cross on the white lorry. The taxi driver was bleeding profusely.

'What happened? What happened?'

The policemen stood still and silent in the confusion watching their colleagues measure the road and cross-examine passers-by. Traffic was already beginning to flow. Just another accident: too many cars in Lagos, the people concluded. But not so for the man who in the ambulance was watching the slight movements of Lilli's lips. She was recovering consciousness. He leaned forward to touch Joe's heart, but drew back with a shock.

Joe was dead.

The moment when the crumpled car had been over his head and Lilli's – those were the happiest moments of his empty life. While his life ebbed fast, he had held Lilli's hands and made great plans for his only son, Olu.

'Only one thing you can do, Lilli.'

'Yes, dear Joe!'

'Look after him – He – he must not be like me.'

'Like you?' She tried to smile while the blood seeped into her eyes. 'Wha's wrong with you?'

'I have been bad –'

'But I love you.'

'Oh Lilli!'

Those were the last words he had said. Lilli could never tell the story without tears of happiness in her eyes. 'Perhaps it was better that way,' she would add.

That same morning a girl was bending over her suitcases at the railway station. They were new ones which her uncle had just bought for her. There were other people who were clamouring to weigh their baggage, because the Kano train would soon be leaving for Northern Nigeria.

The girl was young: not more than eighteen or nineteen at the most, though she was so tall. Her skin was nearer brown than black. It was clear and her keen eyes looked over the station railings into the distance where a crowd was assembled.

She was curious about that crowd, but she couldn't leave her suitcases unattended, and she hadn't yet bought her ticket and seen to all the formalities necessary for boarding a train. That crowd seemed to her sensational, but then Lagos was a sensational city. There was something about that particular crowd that affected her. Lagos was always full of accidents. Who could tell the person involved this time? She was glad she hadn't been in any accident since she arrived.

'They say somebody was killed,' the people said.

'No!' some said. 'Three people –'

Essi focused her attention on the crowd. She saw the police vans, the ambulance – even the fire brigade.

She bought her ticket, and got herself a good seat in a third-class compartment. If you came early as she had done, you would always get a comfortable seat. Not even her mother had accompanied her to the station this time. Her mission to Lagos had failed. But she had enjoyed her time, thanks to her uncle.

It was after the first night on the train that Essi saw the headlines in a paper being read by a fellow-passenger. 'Killed outright –' they said. 'Survived by a boy, two years old –' Essi was genuinely sorry.

'Such a good boy,' she sighed. 'He was the first man who spoke to me when I got to Lagos. He was so kind to me.' She turned to the other girls who were tugging at the paper. 'If you saw this boy, eh! They called him Fussy Joe. So handsome – and such good manners! You'd like him.'

But they were not listening to Essi.

1. MARTIN LUTHER KING, JR. · *Letter from Birmingham Jail*

2. ALLEN GINSBERG · *Television Was a Baby Crawling Toward That Deathchamber*

3. DAPHNE DU MAURIER · *The Breakthrough*

4. DOROTHY PARKER · *The Custard Heart*

5. *Three Japanese Short Stories*

6. ANAÏS NIN · *The Veiled Woman*

7. GEORGE ORWELL · *Notes on Nationalism*

8. GERTRUDE STEIN · *Food*

9. STANISLAW LEM · *The Three Electroknights*

10. PATRICK KAVANAGH · *The Great Hunger*

11. DANILO KIŠ · *The Legend of the Sleepers*

12. RALPH ELLISON · *The Black Ball*

13. JEAN RHYS · *Till September Petronella*

14. FRANZ KAFKA · *Investigations of a Dog*

15. CLARICE LISPECTOR · *Daydream and Drunkenness of a Young Lady*

16. RYSZARD KAPUŚCIŃSKI · *An Advertisement for Toothpaste*

17. ALBERT CAMUS · *Create Dangerously*

18. JOHN STEINBECK · *The Vigilante*

19. FERNANDO PESSOA · *I Have More Souls Than One*

20. SHIRLEY JACKSON · *The Missing Girl*

21. *Four Russian Short Stories*

22. ITALO CALVINO · *The Distance of the Moon*

23. AUDRE LORDE · *The Master's Tools Will Never Dismantle the Master's House*

24. LEONORA CARRINGTON · *The Skeleton's Holiday*

25. WILLIAM S. BURROUGHS · *The Finger*

26. SAMUEL BECKETT · *The End*

27. KATHY ACKER · *New York City in 1979*

28. CHINUA ACHEBE · *Africa's Tarnished Name*

29. SUSAN SONTAG · *Notes on 'Camp'*

30. JOHN BERGER · *The Red Tenda of Bologna*

31. FRANÇOISE SAGAN · *The Gigolo*

32. CYPRIAN EKWENSI · *Glittering City*

33. JACK KEROUAC · *Piers of the Homeless Night*

34. HANS FALLADA · *Why Do You Wear a Cheap Watch?*

35. TRUMAN CAPOTE · *The Duke in His Domain*

36. SAUL BELLOW · *Leaving the Yellow House*

37. KATHERINE ANNE PORTER · *The Cracked Looking-Glass*

38. JAMES BALDWIN · *Dark Days*

39. GEORGES SIMENON · *Letter to My Mother*

40. WILLIAM CARLOS WILLIAMS · *Death the Barber*

41. BETTY FRIEDAN · *The Problem that Has No Name*

42. FEDERICO GARCÍA LORCA · *The Dialogue of Two Snails*

43. YUKO TSUSHIMA · *Of Dogs and Walls*

44. JAVIER MARÍAS · *Madame du Deffand and the Idiots*

45. CARSON MCCULLERS · *The Haunted Boy*

46. JORGE LUIS BORGES · *The Garden of Forking Paths*

47. ANDY WARHOL · *Fame*

48. PRIMO LEVI · *The Survivor*

49. VLADIMIR NABOKOV · *Lance*

50. WENDELL BERRY · *Why I Am Not Going to Buy a Computer*